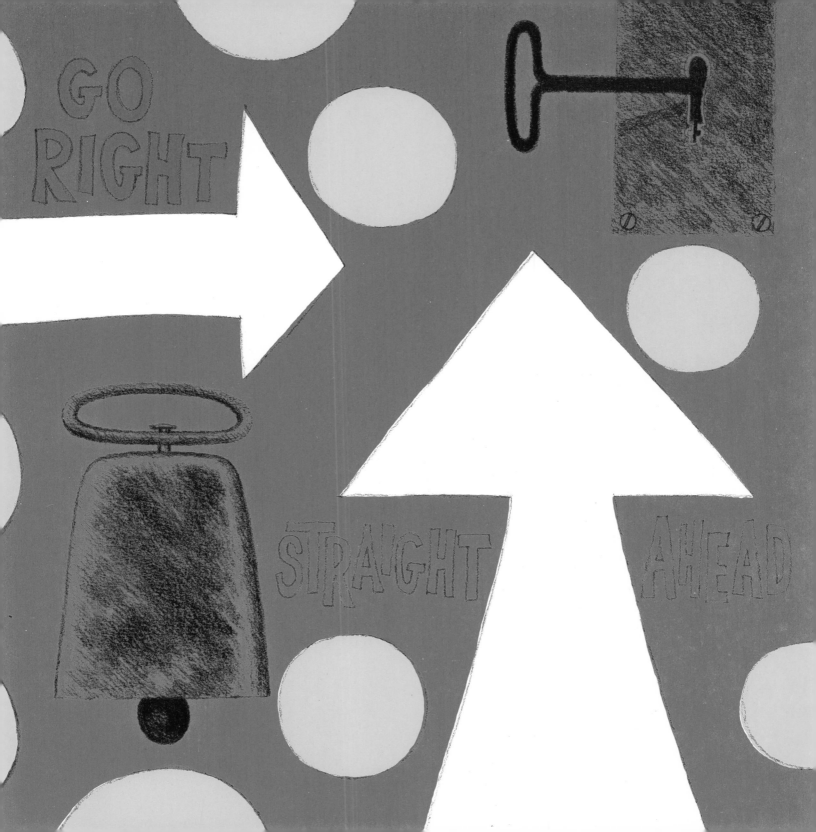

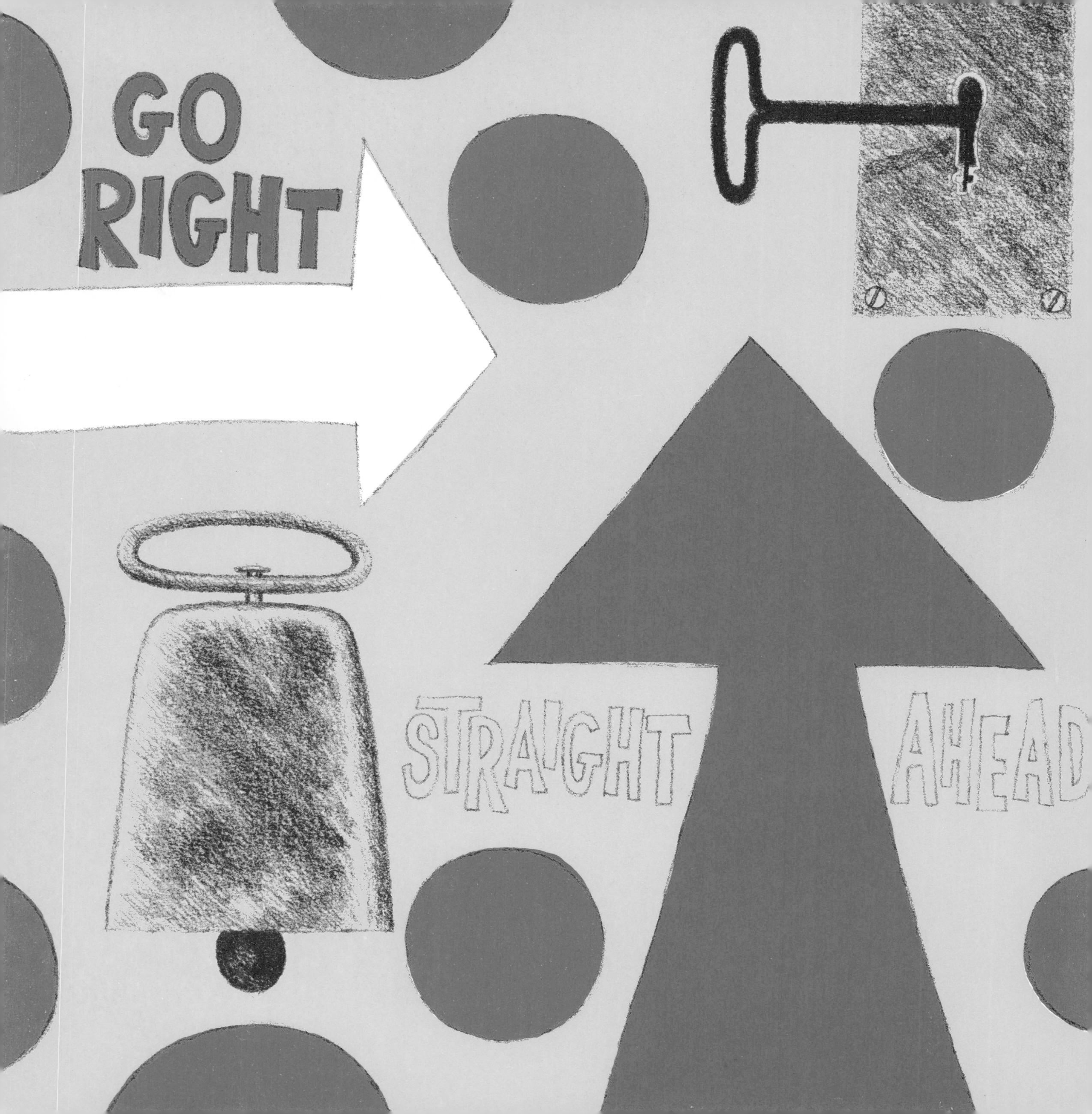
GO
RIGHT
STRAIGHT
AHEAD

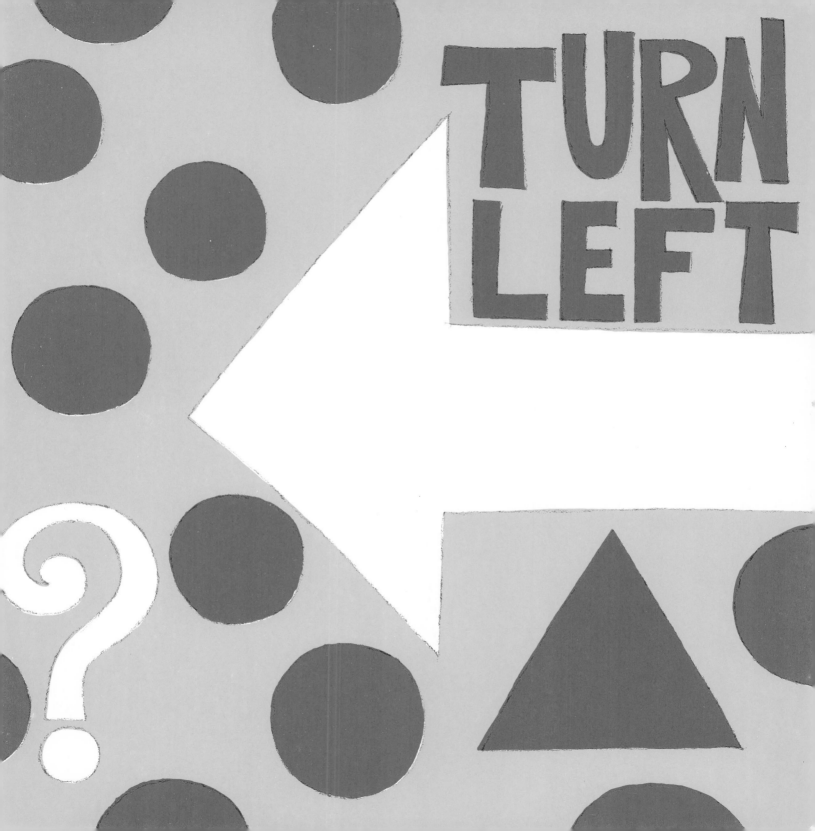

THE
MEDDYBEMPS
FAIR

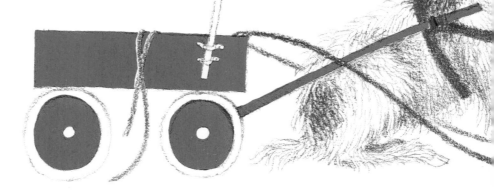

THE MEDDYBEMPS

MEDDYBEMPS
OR
BUSt!

FAIR BY JOHN HOUSTON
PicTURES BY WiNNiE FiTCH
▲ ADDiSON-WESLEY

An Addisonian Press Book

START

Text Copyright © 1973 by John Houston
Illustrations Copyright © 1973 by Winnie Fitch
All Rights Reserved
Addison-Wesley Publishing Company, Inc.
Reading, Massachusetts 01867
Printed in the United States of America
First Printing

Library of Congress Cataloging in Publication Data

Houston, John, 1935—
  The Meddybemps Fair.

  SUMMARY: Describes in verse the special things
to look for on the way to the Meddybemps Fair.

  [1. Stories in rhyme] I. Fitch, Winnie, illus.
II. Title.
PZ8.3.H795Me   [E]   72-7462
ISBN 0-201-02991-X

Come on, let's go to the Meddybemps Fair.
There's lots of good fun for everyone there.

Follow directions and look for the signs.
We'll have a good time,
on our way to the Meddybemps Fair.

First we must look for a mountain
of orange.
What in the world is a mountain of orange?

**Jiminy Jumpkins,
a big pile of pumpkins!**

**Now turn to the left,
on our way to the Meddybemps Fair.**

Now we must listen
for something that's ringing.

**What in the world
could there be here that's ringing?**

Zip, golly, wow, a bell on a cow.
Now turn to the right,
on our way to the Meddybemps Fair.

Now we must look
for some red polka dots.
What in the world could be red polka dots?

Flipples and flapples,
an orchard of apples.

Now, go straight ahead,
on our way to the Meddybemps Fair.

Now we must hunt for a garden of perfume.

What in the world is a garden of perfume?

Fun for our noses,
a garden of roses.

**Now turn to the right,
on our way to the Meddybemps Fair.**

Now we must look for a *key* in a door.
How can we look for a *key* in a door?

Hey, look at "Smo*key*",
a beautiful don*key*.

**Now turn to the left,
on our way to the Meddybemps Fair.**

**Now find a place where the sky disappears.
Where in the world does the sky disappear?**

Over the ridge, an old covered bridge.
Once more to the left,
on our way to the Meddybemps Fair.

Now we must look for a circle of fun.

What in the world is a circle of fun?

Zowee, it's real.
A big ferris wheel.

Hooray, we are here!
We are here at the Meddybemps Fair.
We are here at the Meddybemps Fair!

THE MEDDYBEMPS FAIR

Come on, let's go to the Med — dy — bemps Fair.

There's lots of good fun for every — one there.

Fol—low di — rec–tions and look for the signs. We'll have a good

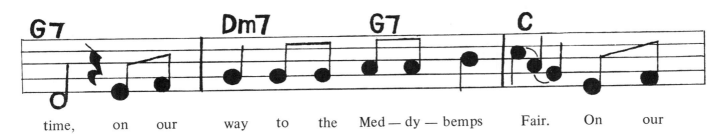

time, on our way to the Med — dy — bemps Fair. On our

way to the Med — dy — bemps Fair.

THE MEDDYBEMPS FAIR:

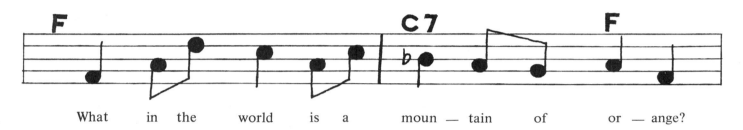

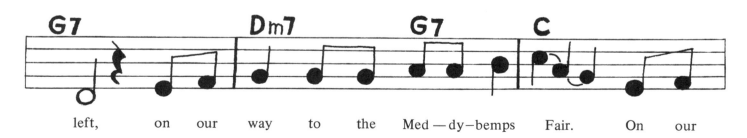

A SONG TO SING · PLAY AND ACT OUT

Now we must listen for something that's ringing.
   What in the world could there be here that's ringing?
Zip, golly, wow, a bell on a cow!
   Now turn to the right, on our way to the Meddybemps Fair.
On our way to the Meddybemps Fair.

Now we must look for some red polka dots.
   What in the world could be red polka dots?
Flipples and flapples, an orchard of apples.
   Now, go straight ahead, on our way to the Meddybemps Fair.
On our way to the Meddybemps Fair.

Now we must hunt for a garden of perfume.
   What in the world is a garden of perfume?
Fun for our noses, a garden of roses.
   Now turn to the right, on our way to the Meddybemps Fair.
On our way to the Meddybemps Fair.

Now we must look for a *key* in a door.
   How can we look for a *key* in a door?
Hey, look at "Smo*key*" a beautiful don*key*.
   Now turn to the left, on our way to the Meddybemps Fair.
On our way to the Meddybemps Fair.

Now find a place where the sky disappears.
   Where in the world does the sky disappear?
Over the ridge, an old covered bridge.
   Once more to the left, on our way to the Meddybemps Fair.
On our way to the Meddybemps Fair.

Now we must look for a circle of fun.
   What in the world is a circle of fun?
Zowee, it's real. A big ferris wheel.
   Hooray, we are here! We are here at the Meddybemps Fair.
We are here at the Meddybemps Fair!

GO
RIGHT

STRAIGHT AHEAD